A Bad Day for

FRANK KUPPNER

A Bad Day for the Sung Dynasty

Copyright © Frank Kuppner 1984

All rights reserved.

First published in 1984 by
Carcanet Press Limited
208-212 Corn Exchange
Manchester M4 3BQ

British Library Cataloguing in Publication Data
    Kuppner, Frank
        A bad day for the Sung Dynasty.
        I. Title
        821'.914   PR6061.U/

    ISBN 0-85635-514-3

The publisher acknowledges the financial assistance of the Arts Council of Great Britain.

Printed in England by SRP Ltd., Exeter

CONTENTS

A Technical Note   1

    I.
A Bad Day for the Sung Dynasty   5

    II.
Soft Laughter and Distant Music   33

    III.
Yellow River Dreaming   61

    IV.
The Moment Passes   89

    V.
The Same Laughter, Further Away   117

A TECHNICAL NOTE

    i.
Possibly the simplest type of quatrain
Is the one that runs through four consecutive lines
Without any major interruption in its flow
Until it reaches the almost inevitable conclusion.

    ii.
Then there's the type which pauses with the first line;
The remainder is heaped together after it,
Giving a distinctly unbalanced air to the whole,
Which perhaps explains its comparative rarity.

    iii.
The type which delays its main pause till the second line
Is probably the one to go for if one wants balance;
Theoretically at least, it is easy to see
Why this should exude a classical air of repose.

    iv.
But by far and away the most common of the forms
Which have only one major stop throughout their duration
Is the one which halts at the end of line three;
I am still not entirely certain why this is so.

    v.
Which brings us to those types with *two* internal stops;
These seem less differentiated than the others;
Possibly their main function is the very valuable one
Of allowing monotony a little more space to hide in.

vi.
Or perhaps there is something more significant about them;
Actually, I am not particularly interested
In teasing out technical nuances after the fact;
If I could sleep I would not be writing this.

vii.
I certainly think it would be an act of sheer folly
To ring the changes according to some pre-set plan;
No—wait a moment—I'm doing that just now, am I not?
Ah well, these are rather unusual circumstances.

viii.
Then there is what I think of as the most basic form of them
    all;
I suspect this is the one from which all the others developed;
Notice how the lines tend to get longer in this typus;
I would imagine it's because rhythmic considerations can
    more easily be ignored when all the lines stop.

ix.
Next we can group together a whole company
Of irregular verse-forms, that is all those which stop
In the middle of a line; one can't help thinking
They could easily be made orthodox with very little additional
    work.

x.
And each of the nine schemata assembled here,
All of which stop at the end of the final line,
Has a nearly identical twin which I have not mentioned,
For a moment's thought should be sufficient to show

I

A Bad Day for the Sung Dynasty

1.
The elderly statesman trudges wearily over the bridge;
He was expected in the palace more than twenty-five minutes
   ago;
Surely that is not his penis he holds in his hand?
From the bedroom of a house in Germany I once saw trees
   exactly like that.

2.
So we sit together in a small pavilion, discussing bygone days;
When we need more wine, more wine is brought out to us;
From the house drifts towards us the unmistakable sound of
    sandal upon buttock;
Or is that small building actually itself the house?

3.
He sits at ease in his small riverside pavilion,
Reading a book and listening to the willows sigh;
But his boy, carrying something, has halted on the nearby
    bridge,
Convinced that someone is looking at his back.

4.
Rain is beating upon a dwelling in the mountains
As harshly as it beat earlier this afternoon;
A water buffalo seems to slip on the main road;
Shakespeare's father utters his first cry elsewhere.

5.
A man stands in the corner of his pavilion, gazing over the
    water;
A man stands on a bridge, gazing at someone else's back;
A man, angling in a boat, gazes impassively in front of him;
In a nearby boat, another man gazes into the water.

6.
What is he reading, in that nearly wall-less house of his?
And what does he read, a few trees away, in another house?
A door stands open; has someone newly left that building?
Will he have the nerve to carry out the theft he plans?

7.
The man on the bridge has obviously just lost his memory;
A friend approaches in a small boat from the east;
What mixed emotions will there be in the house tonight
When, trying to strike him, he slips and knocks his head on
    the floor.

8.
The man on the bridge has obviously just lost his memory;
A friend approaches in a small boat from the east;
Whose daughter is wiping a jade tear from her eye,
And begging her husband to finish his soup quietly?

9.
A group of old men gaze eagerly into the water;
A little girl, who ought to be asleep,
Glances furtively out of the window opposite;
In the nearby bed her brother dreams of elephants.

10.
Looking stunningly like that mad geography teacher of mine
    of twenty years ago,
One of the fishermen, with ease, resettles his creel;
The other, chatting volubly, reaches an arm deep into his
    basket;
Feeling a hand grip his own, he hesitates.

11.
The volume lies untouched on the table, still open at the
    same page,
When, after some hours, I return to the library in the evening;
Still he sits unperturbed on the banks of the same stream;
That is probably still a waterfall in the distance.

12.
Mist has reached to the depths of this river valley;
In ornate raiment he stares out into the gloom;
The corpse on the bridge falls immediately into the water;
In the background, the mountains seem to want to change
    places.

13.
The storm has lit the sky to its own design;
The three old men are buffeted by it as they cross the bridge;
Angry words about verisimilitude flash between them;
The sky reverberates with redoubled fury.

14.
Can it have been to this very tree that he tied her,
Long years ago, to this warped and blackened tree?
He closes his eyes, in a voluptuous daze,
And dances, dances, over the side of the precipice.

15.
Two insects descend onto the head of the great man;
They gaze wistfully across the bald expanse;
Slowly, they begin to edge towards each other;
His sudden cry of understanding frightens them away.

16.
In this bare landscape, deserted for days around,
A group of envoys whisper by a tree-lined lake;
For a few seconds, above the surface of the water,
A large eye breaks, then, seeing nothing, re-submerges.

17.
He leans against an aslant tree, admiring the incredibly boring lake;
He reminds me that yesterday, as I passed from waiting-room to surgery,
The round-bottomed little dental receptionist leant thus against her low table,
Annihilating anxiety for a moment as she faced a boring wall.

18.
With difficulty he reaches the group of pine-trees at the summit;
Several monasteries hang on the huge mountain curtain behind him;
Noticing the exact tree behind which she pissed in the spring,
He smiles, turns to the sunset, and begins to sing.

19.
Suddenly the dog stands erect in the garden;
Bamboo sprouts tall and elegant behind him;
Who is that person being hacked to pieces on an upper balcony?
This could be a bad day for the Sung Dynasty.

20.
With composure, his hands replace themselves on the zither;
The servants tip-toe, hoping not to disturb him;
Behind the screen, his young wife shivers uncontrollably;
Her tea cools in the bowl placed in the garden.

21.

Entirely deserted, whether river or bay or sea;
Not a house on the single folded peninsula;
The foreground island large enough for only six trees;
From the leaves of one of them, a sound of sniggering.

22.

Entirely deserted, whether river or bay or sea;
Not a house on the single folded peninsula;
The foreground island large enough for only six trees;
Inside the hollowed bark of one a hermit listens.

23.

In the distance, a few charred trees and the roof of a temple;
Across the river from the scene of the explosion,
With superb sang froid he plucks at his stringed instrument;
A descending branch narrowly misses his audience's head.

24.

Enchanted by the artistry of the ch'in player,
The sombreroed fisherman lets his craft drift nearer;
One of the two listeners has raised his right hand;
The man seated in the river may also be listening.

25.

Captivated by the sound of the wind rushing among the trees,
He glances upwards in astonishment
As two of the branches from quite different trees
Approach with a sigh and tie themselves in a knot.

26.
Whose boat is that drifting aimlessly down the river?
In his lacquered retreat, deep in the bowels of the mountain,
He drops her silk back onto her bottom for a moment,
And ponders, with her hand in his mouth, the local rapids.

27.
An ordinary isolated mountain hamlet;
Mist rises thick above the delicate valley;
To the front of the wooded, well-appointed houses
One rubbery tree swings to and fro forever.

28.
In the indiscriminate land between land and water,
He plies his rod at the very edge of the earth;
For hour after hour gazing at emptiness,
While the flames gather in his house in the capital.

29.
He plies his rod at the very rim of the earth,
For hour after hour gazing at emptiness
While rebels fire street after street in the capital;
His boy is half asleep in the back of the boat.

30.
The thrush is singing out a pure clear note
On a branch below which a young girl is lying;
There is no frost there at that time of the year;
The farmers are walking quietly to and from their work.

31.
Those marshlands and hills are totally empty;
The day is overcast, but not yet raining;
When, after an hour, he at last catches a fish,
He looks round quickly to trace the source of the sniggering.

32.
The poet relaxes beside a picture on the wall;
The picture shows a man relaxing in front of a picture;
The second picture shows a young lady with naked feet;
With a smile, she extends a hand towards the poet.

33.
A tiny, tiny horse is running towards the Emperor;
He watches it indolently, his expression somewhat bored;
A swarthy court official claps his hands with delight;
The conjuror is escorted out towards the women's quarters.

34.
The lights blaze in the little house by the river;
The three women sit in the boat, waiting;
How long is it now since she was taken into the house?
They listen to the cries of delight with irritation.

35.
Bald-domed, absurdly browed, wild-haired, and long-nosed,
Suddenly they burst into the delicate Yüan courts,
Our ancestors, trailing a huge mastiff for tribute;
So old; so uncouth; I avert my eyes quickly.

36.
The emperor's mistress goes to horse beside the filthy groom;
Every day the rebel troops approach the capital;
He watches her buttocks as she settles in the saddle;
Then they ride off to meet the defending armies.

37.
The emperor stands behind her, correcting her fingering;
Their hands are close; their bodies sway in the same curve;
With joy he hears the music she produces;
Inhaling, exhaling, as she inhales, exhales.

38.
If Newton at this moment is dying in a distant bed,
And a light is now shining through the entire world,
What does he care, that planter of chrysanthemums,
Uttering his own sighs, not final sighs.

39.
A crouching servant picks up a striking stone;
10,000 years before, another eye had examined it;
At a warning cry, it was carelessly replaced;
The servant holding the collecting-bag reaches out.

40.
The poet is elegantly wandering through the woods;
The river is flowing elegantly along beside him;
It is also flowing in a large, rivermouth city;
He is thinking of a dark stairway in that city.

41.
The wind creates new forests in the sky;
An unearthly light gleams in the scholar's house;
Hurriedly his servant covers the hole in the garden;
The sky tries to get through the hole, but he fights it, fights it.

42.
At one time there was a magnificent city here;
A confusion of high palaces and jewelled streets;
Now there is only a marshland and black water,
Two trees, a chair, a lit candle, and some receipts.

43.
With a sigh of contentment he gazes across the river;
He contemplates the intricate cliff opposite;
The cascade, the waterfall, the three separate forests,
From which two pairs of eyes watch him intently.

44.
For the entire morning, I have been vaguely uneasy,
Drinking tea and glancing down the river valley,
To a single bare peak among five snow-capped ones,
Wondering who has had the authority to clear it.

45.
For the entire morning, I have been vaguely uneasy,
Drinking tea and glancing down the river valley,
To a single bare peak among six snow-capped ones;
I ask my wife to get up off the floor for a moment.

46.
For the entire morning I have been perfectly happy,
Drinking tea and glancing down the river valley,
Hearing the woman in the bed behind me
Talk in her sleep about sweeping the snow off mountains.

47.
I ask my wife to get out of bed for a moment
To find out how many peaks there are in the valley;
Muttering hoarsely from warmth, she refuses to go;
This is how it starts; I gaze at the ceiling in tears.

48.
Drinking tea, glancing down the river valley
At the six peaks, sensing a deficiency,
I ask my wife to come over from the bed to join me;
Quietly she brings her tiny trembling peaks towards me.

49.
Every morning when I look out I see more rocks in the river;
When first I came here it was smooth, perfectly smooth;
I don't know how, but I'm sure I am to blame;
I shall go into town tomorrow and consult my doctor.

50.
What has happened to the other half of that mountain?
A hunchback crosses the bridge, laughing mischievously;
The old lady who has fainted on the floor of her cottage,
Feeling her face being kissed, pretends not to wake up.

51.
All those mountains are exactly the same shape;
Surely in fact they are merely the same mountain repeated;
The pilgrim climbing laboriously to the temple on a peak,
Staggers at the top, to see it on the peak in front.

52.
The houses are slowly slipping into the river;
The people are all on the other side of the island
About to realize they have been misinformed;
No, wait a moment: the houses are coming back.

53.
Is that a mountain or a sleeping watchdog?
One half expects such sinuous lines to growl.
The occupant of the only house in the thin valley
Comes out, looks around, then re-enters the house, puzzled.

54.
A huge sculpted phallus has been placed on the flat peak
    overnight,
On a road in the valley two friends meander sedately;
Which of the pair will be the first to draw attention to it?
They meander sedately down a road in the valley.

55.
He cowers in an open corner of his house;
That crane outside is speaking in his wife's voice;
A huge grinning skull has usurped his favourite mountain;
The crane approaches, talking about unhappiness.

56.
The traveller stops in the road in astonishment;
He has just noticed his dead father in a woodland clearing;
His father gazes from the clearing in astonishment
At his dead son gazing at him in astonishment.

57.
The traveller stops in the road in astonishment;
Coming towards him is his brother, whom he poisoned;
His brother stops in the road in astonishment;
Coming towards him is his brother, whom he poisoned.

58.
The two old men amble along the road,
Placidly discussing why neither has ever married;
One quietly pulls back a sleeve, and reveals a third eye;
His companion laughs, and they walk on together in silence.

59.
A pair of exquisite magnolias grow by the side of the road;
He plucks the one which is already in full blossom,
And tosses it through the window-screen of the woman he adores;
Four days later, the other is in full blossom.

60.
They sit together chatting, taking their tea;
Their talk flits lightly over the affairs of the village;
One of them contorts himself into a yawn;
His stretching hand brushes against the Great Wall.

61.
A horizontal crease in the mountains across the river;
Someone has folded and then unfolded them;
The scholar in his study wrinkles his brow,
Then returns to writing his letter of complaint.

62.
A large city and a lake with sailing boats
On a wide plain on top of impassable mountains;
In his cottage in the valley, the guide awakens and frowns;
Still he cannot remember where the single path is.

63.
Mountains above; mountains below; mountains beside;
Mountains between; mountains among; mountains within;
Shout the word 'rain' into the echoing valleys,
For a second the air holds an entire Tempest.

64.
The winter gloom has blackened even the snow;
A bright bird stands inside the small pavilion,
Gazing out at a scene of desolation;
The gloom lifts, and the snow develops voices.

65.
Ever since that day when she threw his gift into the cesspit,
The sight of white poppies always depresses him;
As he struggles to leave their gardens with his eyes shut,
His friends regard him more coolly than before.

66.
No city beyond those mountains for a week's journey;
Three fishermen return home in a misty evening;
Only a brief high fence refutes primeval time;
One of the men has a cleaver thrust into his back.

67.
Three heaps of rubble where once the mountains stood;
The chief engineer turns away from the window and sighs;
Some of his negligence will surely be attributed to him;
He shuts the door quietly and hurries towards the new viaduct.

68.
Lost to the knees in mist he gazes up at the sacred peak;
Its broad flat top shows out of a sea of mist;
Absent-mindedly he spits over a gorse-rimmed ridge;
An unprecedented avalanche collapses onto his head.

69. A Faded Inscription
'Arriving very early I knocked vigorously on your door,
But an old lady from a window opposite told me
You were probably gone up the mountain to find a cool place to jerk off in;
Somewhat alarmed by her smile, I hurried away without waiting.'

70.
For fifteen years day and day he has sailed this noble river;
But now, seeing a huge feather floating down towards him,
In a moment he forgets all his experience,
And tosses his grandfather over the side for good luck.

71.
Three fat men wallow luxuriously in the water;
These hot springs are famed for their potency-giving effects;
Before a jade mirror in a tree-lined lane
A woman prods her nose, smiling to herself.

72.
Three fat men luxuriate wallowingly in the water;
These hot springs are famed for their potency-giving effects;
The woman who serves tea in the neighbouring wineshop
Decides to postpone her return home for a little longer.

73.
Quietly he plants sweet flowers in his quiet garden;
His neighbour, hearing his gentle song, smiles in sympathy;
Not far beneath the flowers and his soft footsteps,
His wife is lying, her hands over her face.

74.
To call that stone a stone is not entirely right;
Nor is that narcissus merely a narcissus;
The old scholar, standing on the path, weeping,
Is an old scholar, standing on a path, weeping.

75. *'Leaving Home'. A faded inscription.*
'I swing my staff lustily at the flowers;
I smell the trees of the mountain opposite;
Overhanging a ravine, a pine shakes
Like a farewell salute; in tears I bow to it.'

76. *'Leaving A House'. A faded inscription.*
'The wayside flowers reach up to ensnare my member;
The mountain opposite throws a tree at me;
Remembering an intimate part of her body
As I leave her house, I weep, thinking of my failure.'

77.
There are twenty-five trees in this pleasant valley,
And bats hang upside-down on every one;
The smiling traveller looks curiously around him,
Then decides to stay the night in the previous valley.

78.
The happy fish darts from shadow to shadow;
It believes itself to be an inhabitant of Versailles;
Chinese statesmen wave vaguely at the surface of the water;
The fish chuckles at the sheer *élégance* of it all.

79.
Above the overhang, the Emperor admires the blue sunset;
The court musicians improvise exquisitely;
The lady smiles, shifts a little, and says nothing;
Beneath the overhang, two quails are looking at each other.

80.
A boy is sweeping the garden clear of twigs;
A crane ambles around on the grass behind him;
Reaching a rock, it turns and ambles back;
Reaching a river, it turns and ambles back.

81.
One of the mountains peeps round the side of another
Like a child sheltering behind its mother's gown;
In a garden in the valley within sight of them
A small child is tugging hard at its mother's gown.

82.
The historian gazes out of his window
With a look of sheer ignorance upon his face;
Workmen have appeared round the corner of the river
Quietly replanting flowers all over the road.

83.
Weeds are everywhere around the little lake,
But still the scholar sits by the open window;
Loudly, he calls out one of the serving-girls' names,
Then, remembering what has happened, blushes and is silent.

84.
Mist floods downwards from the peaks and the ravines;
Mist pours thickly down the precipitous valley;
Gathers and pours itself into a small wine-jar
Newly opened by a grinning virgin.

85.
She opens her window and looks out into the morning;
An old man is swaying drunkenly on the bridge;
In a flash she remembers an appalling scene from her youth;
Then, recollecting his death, she turns to smile at her husband.

86.
A huge explosion in the heart of the mountain;
In the temple, the praying monks are subtly displaced;
In horror, emerging from their meditations
To discover the sky far too close beside them.

87.
It is a hard thing, deliberately to choose a cave
Inaccessible halfway up a cliff to meditate in,
And then glance down one morning in a state of comparative
    bliss
To discover a sea-level below, rising alarmingly.

88.
One of the group of guards left behind at the archway,
Stretching his neck in bored indifference,
Catches ships floating by in the sky above him;
From that day on, the number of deserters grew.

89.
The fishermen trudging wearily home in the evening
Hear behind them the sound of the mountain temple
Lifting off towards the depths of the sky;
Looking over their shoulders, they continue to trudge.

90.
The cascade gives up halfway through its fall;
Beside it, in a nest in a tree, sit two philosophers;
With a sudden snap, their branch falls into the river;
They float on untroubled, discussing déjà vu.

91.
The distinctive, bulbous shape of Frog Head Mountain
Haunts his dreams as he sways in his hotel bed;
A long, sticky tongue probes through the open window;
It licks his face, almost causing him to awake.

92.
He throws open the shutters on a superb autumn morning;
Inhaling deeply, he gazes out at the golden land;
It is true a regular breathing sound is drifting down from the
    mountains,
But he confuses it with the rustling of the leaves around him.

93.
Deserted, wet, barren, absent of life,
This stubbed plain lies between nowhere and nowhere;
Yet, if last month a letter had not been intercepted,
The dust of 500,000 horsemen would now be settling in it.

94.
In his grandfather's time, hordes screamed through that pass there;
Now he sits in the still study looking out at the pines;
He hears his wife's resolute step approaching in the passage-way;
Trembling a little, he continues to look at the pines.

95.
A stately enemy fleet sails into the bay;
From the watch-tower the guards look down expectantly;
For seventeen years the fleet stays anchored there;
In his cabin the captain leans studiously over his plans.

96. *An Inscription*
'Let us, while youth endures, visit these river pavilions,
Opening our wine bottles as the boats pass swiftly,
To discover less inside than we had anticipated,
Thereby beginning to suspect the truth about our mothers.'

97.
What has happened to the man riding the donkey?
He was seen entering this valley in the morning,
But, by the evening, he had not been seen to leave,
And now the river is flowing in the wrong direction.

98.
Concealed in the quest for unsuspicious birds,
Despite the misty cold, he at length falls asleep,
Waking to find himself transported by talons,
Above a landscape of hunters laughing in their sleep.

99.
Every thirty seconds a rider arrives and disappears
Into the small shack beside the one tree in the plain;
All day this has happened, with no one ever exiting;
The aged shepherd begins to stroll towards the building.

100.
Two isolated temples in neighbouring valleys;
No other building within a day's journey;
The monks are gazing ecstatically at the landscape,
Neither group knowing of the other's existence.

II

*Soft Laughter
and Distant Music*

101.
The two friends arranged they would meet here after the war,
At this out-of-the-way wineshop, if they survived;
Now drunk, they loll in neighbouring cubicles,
Each tearfully lamenting the other's death.

102.
An incessant powder has fallen during the night;
All has been covered in black, even the river;
How many cities have the rebels burned by now,
The woodsmen wonder, wiping their wives clean.

103.
A man stands at a small confluence, listening to the water;
The slightest push would topple him into the river;
A servant stands behind him, his arms full of luggage;
At night one sleeps peacefully and one lies awake.

104.
For generations children have played upon those heights,
And have slid down those steep slopes towards their homes;
Now the whole region is entirely under water;
Some children are plying their boats upon the water.

105. *An Inscription*
'This morning, realizing I am sixty-five years old,
And have still not touched my neighbour's unmarried sister,
Except fleetingly, by accident, seventeen years ago,
I throw a furtive stone at his head as he strolls in his garden.'

106.
The drunken poet falls asleep beneath the tree,
And when he awakens, it is the tree which is drunk,
And the moon which is drunk, and the river which is drunk,
And he starts, perfectly sober, to walk home backwards.

107.
A row of soldiers crosses the bridge in the valley;
A column of horses clings to a high path;
Two ladies, drinking tea in their pavilion,
Gulp, as a line of bodies falls past their windows.

108.
All day, the two boats have raced each other up the river;
On the deck of one, three men are fighting to the death;
On the other, a woman dances in front of a child;
The townspeople eagerly anticipate their arrival.

109.
The lady, leaning on her warming brazier, smiles;
How often did he tell her she is fascinating?
Perhaps, in less than an hour, they will meet again;
The servant-girl, standing by the candle, smiles.

110.
A servant-girl is sweeping a palace pathway;
Her mistress walks through the river on marble slabs;
Every year, the wilderness encroaches further;
Already, unknown fish live in the pool.

111.
They are bringing in supplies to store during the winter;
One carries a huge pannier of rice upon his shoulders;
Another, two baskets of rice yoked round his neck;
Another carries a young girl under his arm.

112.
Coming down the quiet lane, he glances through a doorway;
A smiling girl has slumped over a table;
She holds her left hand in a curious shape, and looks at it;
He walks on, investigating his own left hand.

113.
Secure as the leaves fly about his pavilion,
Complacently he watches the storm raging;
Sitting as he is, with his back to the nearby mountain,
He is not well positioned to see the wave run over it.

114.
The river meanders quietly out of the gaseous mountains,
Taking no trouble to disguise or to exaggerate its strength;
If it must drown more people, it will drown more people;
It no longer has to prove itself to anybody.

115.
The crane reaches out its claws and moves a rook;
In despair, the conjuror clasps a hand to his forehead;
In a few thrusts, his defence has been ripped to tatters;
He glowers at his calmly smiling opponent.

116.
The old painter suddenly sits bolt upright in the garden;
Can he really have spent the last eighty years
Painting nothing but tufts of bamboo by riversides?
Quietly he keels over onto the grass.

117.
He holds his big authoritative hand up in the air;
She holds out her tiny hand, clenched and pointing;
A pliant branch bends in the cool alcove;
One of them, with eyes closed, is smiling happily.

118.
A man is beating a cliff-face with a stick;
He is not mad; he is not even enraged;
After a while, he stops it and goes away;
On returning home, he finds that his wife is awake.

119.
A sudden silence beneath the boat canopy;
Drifting on the lake, they stare at the distant shore;
Something like a large wooden horse stands opposite them;
One of them is vaguely reminded of something.

120. *An Inscription*
'For five hours I climbed this mountain pillar,
Visiting your small hut in a plateaued forest,
To find a note stuck to your door saying,
You were gone for a month to a brothel in the provincial
    capital.'

121.
The old lady is pointedly biting her fingers;
The middle lady smilingly pulls at an ear;
The youngest lady has placed a hand on her stomach;
The rent-collector quakes inwardly as he eats the apple.

122.
Sitting at the foot of a thunderous waterfall,
Gazing across at tumultuous mountain pillars,
The philosopher shuts his eyes and strikes his forehead,
Realizing he is thinking of absolutely nothing.

123.
Sitting at the foot of a thunderous waterfall,
Gazing across at tumultuous mountain pillars,
The philosopher shuts his eyes and strikes his chest,
Realizing he is thinking of her again.

124.
In the topmost room of a house precariously perched
On a ragged pinnacle jutting out of the sea,
Connected to the mainland by a leaping wooden bridge,
She stares at the jagged waves, trying to stay awake.

125.
Weeping at his door, he glances at the mountain opposite;
Again he notices that tree-lined road, high up.
Yet, no matter what paths he has followed into that cliff,
He has never once reached that avenue of trees.

126.
Since moving to a house at the mouth of this wondrous valley,
Every morning he has flung the window open,
Hoping to see a view utterly devoid of people;
But once again someone is standing on the bridge.

127.
Clearing a drawer, he finds it and takes it out;
This pebble has been handed from father to son so often
That no one now remembers its significance;
By the way, it exactly models one of the asteroids.

128.
The last time he reached this confluence of rivers,
Impulsively, he forced his way along the other current,
Unplanned, seeking adventure in its unknown land;
This time he drifts past it with a smile on his face.

129.
The last time he reached this confluence of rivers,
Impulsively, he forced his way along the other current,
Unplanned, seeking adventure in its unknown land;
This time he drifts past it with a scowl on his face.

130.
At sunrise, the river's waves grow more excited;
The waterfall leaps into it with increased joy;
The young sisters washing themselves in the inlet
Hurry onto the land and look behind themselves trembling.

131.
He reaches from his bed and lifts the corner of the curtain;
A bad, wet day; he glances at the river anxiously;
She paddles on her hands and knees in the inlet below his window;
He smiles, throws a coin onto the path outside, and sleeps.

132.
As we climbed the high forest, it began to rain heavily;
We were fortunate to find a covered pathway,
With its wooded ceiling and floor, stretching for mile after mile;
We followed its eternity of pillars until the sun came.

133.
Having lived on this small island for seventeen years,
Coming one day round his usual bend in the road,
Looking up at the pagoda on the cliff,
Seeing at last the prearranged signal.

134.
A tiny plug of an island in the night sea;
A momentary shaft of moonlight descending reveals
Three naked figures racing towards a pair of cottages;
From the temple, the sound of an unexpected bell.

135.
The trees struggle up from the ground in unison;
Straining, they flutter their branches, high above the earth;
Some flocks of pinetrees drift off towards the south;
The startled guns report in a thousand valleys.

136.
At the top of a column of rock, a flat plain and trees;
A few boys are having a game of football up there;
From the valley below, their mothers call them home for their dinners;
Laughing amongst themselves, they descend through the trapdoor.

137.
If plausibility were the criterion,
None of the mountains in this view would exist;
A tired traveller might rest on a small eminence,
Beneath that group of pines, not sheer in space.

138.
Struck dumb, a bright light blaring about him,
He lets the letter fall to the table from his shaking hand;
He reaches out unsteadily towards the wine bottle;
Inland she too is drinking wine at this moment.

139.
Struck dumb, a bright light blaring about him,
He lets the letter fall to the table from his shaking hand;
A brisk wind lifts it and takes it outside the villa,
Blowing it past the library window where I sit writing.

140.
The man crossing the small arched bridge is dreaming;
The houses nestling in the inlet are all dreams;
In her dream she strikes a pinetree by the riverside;
The dreaming birds fly out of it towards the small arched bridge.

141.
Two fish glide through the stream in the warm morning;
When an identical warmth next flutters through those peach-trees,
One will have passed down the throat of a young lady,
The other will be being thrown at the governor's inefficient deputy.

142.
Flock after flock sweeps across the river plain,
Making Western letters in a Chinese sky;
The children playing in the garden look up;
The couple arguing in the lane looks up.

143.
When I was a schoolboy, I often drew such identical squiggles
To delineate birds (usually circling battleships);
Now, years later, I observe thirteen such flicks of the wrist
Filing past a pavilion towards some Chinese ships.

144.
When a schoolboy, I drew birds with such identical squiggles;
Now, twenty years later, I observe such flicks of the wrist
Filing past a pavilion towards some Chinese ships,
Floating five centuries before my childish battleships.

145.
The visitor nonchalantly picks the stone up from the sill;
Still talking, he tosses it carelessly in the air;
The host reaches out, catches it, replaces it;
The conversation flows on uninterrupted.

146.
The visitor nonchalantly picks the stone up from the sill;
Still talking, he tosses it carelessly into the air;
The young girl crouching under the unvisited bridge
Is astonished when it lands beside her feet.

147.
The visitor carelessly picks the stone up from the sill;
Still talking, he tosses it nonchalantly into the air;
When he catches it, it seems twice its previous weight;
He replaces it quietly, and continues talking.

148.
The visitor nonchalantly picks the stone up from the sill;
Still talking, he tosses it carelessly into the air;
A brief flurry of liquid descends on him in its place;
His host sits unseeing, blinded by the sun.

149.
The visitor nonchalantly picks the stone up from the sill;
Still talking, he tosses it carelessly into the air;
It reaches its highest point, but does not fall;
The conversation flows on uninterrupted.

150.
The visitor nonchalantly picks the stone up from the sill;
He throws it carelessly into the air and catches it;
With a deft reversal, it then throws the visitor into the air;
The host and the stone smile knowingly at each other.

151.
He stands mournfully at the edge of the stream beside his
 house;
A minute ago, in a rage, he threw a manuscript into the river;
If only he had waited, or had lived further from a stream;
He trudges back to the house, trying to remember the first line.

152.
Seeing the girl at the casement the traveller waves to her;
She disappears inside the house;
The traveller instinctively quickens his pace;
When she peeps back out of the window he has gone entirely.

153.
From a small house in the valley, the sound of flute-playing;
Every night of a hundred, the same mournful music;
As night settles down, and the wailing continues,
A figure carrying a trowel slips across a nearby bridge.

154.
A fearsome groan from behind the obscured treestump;
Can they be rescuing footsteps in the distance?
The thieves by this time have reached their mother's house;
Exploding with relief, they invent nicknames for the dog.

155.
A stupendous fire is sweeping towards the town;
In panic, the occupants flee towards the river;
In greater panic, the houses flee past the occupants;
Unconsciously the occupants slow down a little.

156.
At first light he hurries into the garden,
To a heap of leaves fallen about his mango tree,
Searching for the one that yesterday she bit;
His cries of joy influence the neighbour's dream.

157.
The sedate scholar on his flamboyant donkey
Is thinking of his reception in the palace
As he rides beneath an exquisite overhanging branch
Out of which drops a whispering ruffian.

158.
The scholar drinking wine in his mountain hideaway
Has assumed an untypical expression of fear;
Is it the terrace he sits upon that is rising
Or the huge straight peak opposite him that is falling?

159.
The last time he reached this confluence of rivers,
Impulsively he forced his way along the other current,
Unplanned, seeking adventure in its unknown land;
This time, asleep, he sails past without noticing it.

160.
In all the world, that one clump of trees is magnetic;
It alone retains the sounds that it has heard;
One winter, when the cottage-dweller chops them down, and
    throws them piecemeal into his fire,
He hears so much soft laughter and distant music.

161.
At first I thought it was the moon behind that plumtree,
Now I realize it is more likely to be a mere hole in the fabric
    of the picture itself;
Outside the window, low grey clouds and an incessant fine rain;
The moon is over America, drifting towards the plumtrees.

162.
Eyes which are only flowers look out from behind the banana
    plant;
Eyes which are only damp patches look out from the rock
    above;
The cock in the foreground stares piercingly, but is merely
    pigment;
Only much later did I notice a bird high up in the tree.

163.
Behind him towers a huge mountain, like an explosion;
The valley careers away frighteningly into the mist;
He sits in the garden of an immense brooding monastery,
Making his sixth drawing of a swaying cluster of pomegranates.

164.
Lazily the lotuses wave by the riverbank;
A distant angler worries about impending madness;
The duck floating serenely down the stream
Sings into the microphone among the lilypads.

165.
Eyes half shut, the master fingers the long neck of his lute;
A servant boy approaches, holding a long-spouted jar;
Another servant abstractedly waves a long-necked fan;
A garden-stone with six holes in it obscures them from the
　　public highway.

166.
For a full day they have played their elaborate boardgame;
Beside them, two servants gaze at each other longingly;
An onlooker rests his chin on an elaborately lacquered fan;
One of the servants whispers to the other.

167.
For a full day they have played their elaborate boardgame;
Whichever phoenix first stalls the haihiatus wins outright;
Each player has staked his whole estate on the outcome;
Neither notices the onlooker's eyes suddenly widen.

168.
The poets are discussing great questions on the palace terraces;
Some ladies stand round, offering wine and understanding;
Creeping across a plank-bridge nearby, shrouding her face,
The Empress's sister returns bruised from the city.

169.
Last year they swore they would all reassemble
In the same place when the day came round again;
And so now the moon, because of a drunken vow,
Lights up five people, clambering on the roof of a palace.

170.
With hand raised in ecstasy, he listens to her playing the harp;
The smile on his face is almost identical to the smile on hers;
The cascade of her delicate hands fills the whole of the room
    with music;
Unable to see the music, he instead smiles at her hands.

171.
Among elegant furniture and a pretty girl,
He sits on a dais, smiling contentedly as he writes;
One feels one is looking at a very happy man;
Someone has inscribed his epitaph in the space above his head.

172.
The riverbank is almost wide enough to be an estuary;
The whole view breathes a spirit of pure emptiness;
One might think the scene a desert, except that, in the fore-
    ground,
A young lady is fastened to one of the inner walls of the
    pavilion.

173.
So thin a river it can hardly hold the three boats;
A child, alone on the skiff not far from the bank,
Abstractedly draws a piece of cloth through the water,
Wondering when either parent is going to resurface.

174.
So thin a river it can scarcely contain the three boats;
A group of fishermen snigger triumphantly
Towards a young girl holding a bird in her hands;
Slowly the drops of blood fall from her fingers.

175.
So thin a river it can scarcely contain the three boats;
The mother sits contentedly watching the young boy eat;
Of course he can observe that she is exposing herself,
But the idea does not cross his mind in quite that form.

176.
They sit in their boat near a bemused fisherman;
The woman smiles happily at the young boy plying his chopsticks;
It has of course crossed his mind that she has been exposing herself;
But adulthood is a sufficient explanation of that.

177.
So much activity on the road through the village;
Almost all the male villagers surround two fighting cocks;
The yells of the strident men and silent wildfowl mingle,
Awakening at once any of the women who are sleeping.

178.
In one hand he grips a writhing, exultant snake;
In another hand he holds an exquisitely played flute;
In another hand he clasps an even more venomous snake;
A huge crowd has gathered in the city lane.

179.
Hearing the sound of horses crossing the bridge,
They look down, but the bridge is wholly unoccupied;
Nearby, some horsemen are approaching it at great speed;
Looking out, in surprise, they recognize their own horses.

180.
Eyes closed, the arhat sits, lost in meditation;
A stegosaurus comes round from the rock behind him,
So heavy-footed it breaks into his reverie;
The arhat looks, then closes his eyes again.

181. *An Inscription on a Wine-Bowl*
'From a dream in which the goddess of knowledge kissed me
Chastely on the forehead, and bade me go on a special mission,
I am wakened into a wine-soaked early dawn
By the landlord's mother tenderly licking my nose.'

182.
With a yell of triumph he finishes the great work;
He slumps back in his seat, exhausted but happy;
Idly, he fingers through it, and reads the very first lines;
Little by little the smile disappears from his face.

183.
An unearthly light shines from inside the cave;
The man stands hesitating by the entrance;
Yesterday, there with him, she lost a hairpin on the ground;
Bitterly he regrets volunteering to return to find it.

184.
It was in this cavernous and hooded valley
That the first Chinese attempts at man-powered flight took
    place;
Really, they could hardly have chosen a worse location;
It is more or less impossible to invent flight near pagodas.

185.
With arms folded, the man stands grimly determined at the
    prow of the skiff;
Behind him, a crane marches up and down morosely;
At the rear, a menial trains a machine-gun at the river;
The carp are going to pay pretty severely for this insult.

186.
The cancerous black slick is spreading through the bay;
For years now the land has been abandoned;
A black liquid continues to ooze down from the trees;
In the lakeside pavilion, a few crumpled papers rustle.

187.
The ridge reminiscent of a human hip-skeleton,
And the soft mountain an oddly nippled protrusion;
The drunkards in the riverside pavilion
Gaze away from the dancing girl, then back to her.

188.
A thick crowd is filling the busy shopping street;
The shopkeepers sit benignantly beneath their shutters;
No one whatever shops in the adjacent street;
But a crowd is racing either towards it or away from it, across
    a bridge.

189.
The photograph of the wall of the tomb includes some of the
    muddy ground;
There seem to be some footsteps at its very base;
A painted sheep stands above, its hooves eroded away;
Obviously the photographer did not go near enough to it.

190.
An elegant cart whirrs along the wide street;
Automatically the pedestrians adapt to it;
Neither of the men on board it in fact possesses a face;
But most are too intent on their own business to notice this.

191.
Plates spin juggle and twist, balls fly in clusters;
The king indulgently observes their trained antics;
When the panda plummets from the high pole,
The courtiers relax at the glimpse of regal amusement.

192.
Plates spin juggle and twist, balls fly in clusters;
The king indulgently observes their trained antics;
When the panda plummets from the high pole,
He stretches out a leisurely hand and catches it.

193.
Dutifully listening to the four expert musicians
Who are welcoming at length an important visitor to his court,
The king manages to retain his austere smile
By imagining them pissing on his guest from a considerable
    height.

194.
In his private apartments the Emperor relaxes;
He has tied his hair to the wrist of a zither-player;
When she reaches for the low notes, a pain racks his whole
    being,
But the three little hands around his neck prevent him from
    moving forward.

195.
After the ordeal, the Emperor relaxes;
One of the twins rubs her eyebrows against his forehead;
The other rubs her forehead against his eyebrows;
Their mother sings old songs of her native land.

196.
After his grim ordeal the Emperor relaxes;
Two nude female musicians play impeccable lute music,
While a third, wearing a tiny leather jacket,
Leans out of a window and describes what birds she can see.

197.
After his appalling ordeal, the Emperor relaxes;
One of the triplets places a foot upon his forehead;
Another runs at full speed towards the window;
The third sings softly inside her mother's body.

198.
After his devastating ordeal, the Emperor relaxes;
Whenever the cook strikes the drum with her little bottom,
The giggling musicians, with practised agility,
Scatter to avoid the next of her cakes he throws at them.

199.
After his cataclysmic ordeal, the Emperor relaxes;
With a puzzled smile, he shines a torch upon their mother,
While the quadruplets dance to the rhythm of his heart,
Three of them balanced upon disgraced ambassadors.

200.
After fifty years of frantic and unplanned travelling,
He finds himself outside the house where he wrote his first
 poem;
The stream still flows by as flippantly as ever;
He hears some running feet, and a door shutting.

III

Yellow River Dreaming

201.
In stances familiar from photographs of modern golfers,
Two men on an old stamped tile go about their harvesting;
Above their heads swim fish as large as themselves;
The left-hand side of the stone has been badly chipped.

202.
A vast feast reconstructed upon the walls;
A group of headless actors entertain the visiting dignitaries;
At the left wall, a huge table, filled with delicacies;
At the right wall, another huge table, with a cat running
    along it.

203.
How like an X-ray those bamboo stalks look;
They sit together, demurely talking of cabbages;
But through the window, those ghosts of human limbs
Writhe and conjoin in all sorts of passionate attitudes.

204.
When, on the third morning after the marriage,
He rushed out immediately after breakfast
To observe a waterfall, the young bride
Began to suspect the quality of his poetry.

205.
Rome faltered as that picture was being painted,
And the avenues had already been trailed flat;
A fine brush is thoughtfully drawn across coarse silk;
Oh, all our pictures, our millions of fine pictures.

206.
It seems, the older the picture, the bigger the crowds;
Why do they so hurry towards the reception?
A tremor in the leaves is the fall of Rome,
Drowned out by the shutting of an official's door.

207.
Arrayed in neat rows, the orchestra sounds luminously;
In front of them a tall naked dancer gyrates in feigned distress;
An appreciative whisper shimmers through the audience;
Probably gratitude for the subtlety of their culture.

208.
One coach follows the next down the vast tree-lined avenue;
A group of outriders prances in perfect unison;
Damp has seeped down from the top of the tomb wall;
A stray horse scurries away from a crack in the roadway.

209.
Apparently young ladies adorning themselves with jewels;
A few scrapes of old paint still remain on the slab;
Youthful vanity deciphered like a dead language;
Not many girls here in the library today, I see.

210.
For five hours he has voyaged through the palace corridors,
Trying to find a return to the streets outside;
Dare he ask this high official, or would that be a gross social blunder?
In submissive posture, he lets the Imperial Rabbit Delouser pass.

211.
A girl stands on a riverbank, flagellating herself;
A chorus of old men approach stealthily stage right;
No, wait a moment: they are in the picture below;
And, of course, the girl is not really flagellating herself.

212.
A girl stands by the riverside, really flagellating herself;
The Emperor watches with a tense expression;
The lady holding his sunshade is about to faint;
Slowly the monster begins to climb down the rocks.

213.
For hour after hour, the court ladies prepare their hair;
For hour after hour gaze soulfully at their own faces,
Preparing their entrancing conversation,
Unaware of the Emperor's member thrusting through a hole in their ceiling.

214.
When, finally, maddened by months of sheer neglect,
The court lady waylays the Emperor in his private garden,
Showing her teeth, and insisting on being sent home,
She for the first time realizes that he is in fact a monkey.

215.
As the two officials converse on a palace stairway,
Each has, as convention demands, a female servant standing behind him,
Holding her right hand delicately over his anus;
The origins of this custom are lost in antiquity.

216.
As the two officials converse on a palace stairway,
Each has, as convention demands, a female servant standing behind him,
Holding her left hand delicately against his anus;
Visitors were startled at first, but very soon grew used to it.

217.
As the two officials converse on a palace stairway,
Each has, as convention demands, a female servant standing in front of him,
Against whose anus he delicately places an index finger;
They complain in low tones about the recent deplorable changes.

218.
As the two officials converse on a palace stairway,
Each has, as convention demands, five female servants in front of him,
And another five female servants standing behind him;
The guide to court etiquette now fills many large volumes.

219.
The servants in the courtyard desperately fight the flames;
He lifts up his mother's coffin and carries it from the blazing house;
Outside, he finds himself in a medieval Italian village;
He gazes at the mute face of his mother, fighting back the tears.

220.
In the morning he clambered out of a stinking well,
And by the evening he was sleeping between two princesses;
Under those circumstances, what else could a man dream about?
Though both the girls are silent, neither is asleep.

221.
Buried in haste during the flight from the capital,
The treasure of the dynasty rests in a shallow grave,
Unsuspected by the young woman lying on top of it,
Sobbing at the unexpected course her life has just taken.

222.
All these saints look much the same anywhere,
But I am surprised by the picture of the Chinese knights in mail;
Now, if a certain English king had been pierced in the eye by one of *their* arrows,
I would probably not have bought, earlier this afternoon, a tape of Orlando Gibbons' music.

223.
A flotilla of foreign ships is visiting the harbour today;
People with strange eyes and noses descend from them,
Talking in strange uncelestial gutturals,
And strangely able to distinguish men from women.

224.
The huge chieftain writhes in utter misery;
A dozen restraining hands seek to placate him;
Distraught, his musicians and dancers collapse at the foot of his bed;
In the twenty previous years, he had never once noticed a wrong note before.

225.
That man is chasing a tiger; this man is chasing a tiger;
The group of four men over there is chasing a tiger;
I see a tiger down there; another one must be on the hill somewhere;
So who is he, sitting in the centre of the picture, playing a flute?

226.
I'm very sorry; I don't particularly mean to give offence;
I'm sure it's only due to the poor state of the original;
But that Buddha there appears surely to be masturbating;
Certainly, his expression does nothing to dispel the misconception.

227.
The long pendulous misshapen ears of Amitābha
Vaguely recall a figure I have seen in a television science fiction show;
But his ears were misshapen in a different way;
I believe he published his autobiography a few years back.

228.
In paradise, the collection of Buddhist sages,
Sitting in groups below stupendous pagodas,
With an expression of serenity on all faces,
Try to ignore a recent, unusually durable fart.

229.
The vast armies regard each other warily;
The generals compete in expressions of hauteur;
By dusk, as the walls of the fort vibrate to their groans,
The left kneecap of the Buddha will have changed possession.

230.
For a full minute he stands enraptured before the newly discovered wall painting;
It is for this that for months he has investigated these caves;
Turning to retrace his steps, he is brought to a halt,
By the row of shoes neatly lining the far wall.

231.
Perspiring, the sorcerer performs in front of the Emperor;
Where has the favourite concubine disappeared to?
Trying to stay calm, he lifts up box after box,
But each of them is empty, save for a few hairs.

232,
The horse kneels, seemingly overcome by grief;
The groom holds his hands to his eyes, seemingly distracted;
The prince holds his hand to his chin, seemingly resolute;
Needless to say, things are not what they seem.

233.
The horse kneels, seemingly overcome by grief;
The groom holds his hands to his eyes, seemingly distracted;
The prince holds his hand to his chin, seemingly resolute;
The stream flows by, seemingly inanimate.

234.
The horse kneels, seemingly overcome by grief;
The groom holds his hands to his eyes, seemingly distracted;
The prince holds his hand to his chin, seemingly resolute;
Actually, only one of them is genuine.

235.
Wearily reaching his secret innermost chamber,
The Emperor turns with a smile, and notes with surprise
That twelve previous emperors are already in the room beside him;
Almost his first thought, of course, is to suspect poison.

236.
Wearily reaching his secret innermost chamber,
The Emperor turns with a smile, and notes with surprise
That twelve previous emperors are already in the room beside him;
Wearily he goes out again, to find the new conjuror.

237.
It was always the style with the previous emperor
For two courtiers to stand beside him, holding up his hands;
This one prefers to hear women breathing behind him;
Ugly rumours begin to pervade the palace.

238.
How long does it take an emperor to put all those accoutrements on?
The work of a thousand hands must be about his person.
Strange that so many people should cling to him
As he wanders in solitude through his chamber of mirrors.

239.
The Western ambassadors file in, bearing their tributes:
A blonde, a flying buttress, some Vikings,
A second blonde, Hadrian's Wall, a fake Rembrandt,
A third blonde, a fourth blonde, a fifth blonde.

240.
The Western ambassadors file in, bearing their tributes:
Two blondes, a half-scale model of the Colosseum,
Polyphony, the square root of two, a Greek vase,
A third blonde, a pedometer, a redhead, Individualism.

241.
The Western ambassadors file in, bearing their tributes:
Gunpowder, Fermat's theorem, bamboo,
Printing, Cologne Cathedral (incomplete);
The blond emperor rises to his feet in a rage.

242.
Delegated to decide which old poems should be kept,
And which destroyed, to lessen the excess baggage of time,
In a bad mood, hungover, he burns scroll after scroll,
Hugging his own works to his heart and crooning.

243.
Morosely he gazes at the old text in front of him,
What on earth is he to make of all those absurd squiggly lines?
Something sunlight something something laughter;
Happiness something something something she.

244.
Stolidly he ponders the old text in front of him;
Delight something buttocks pliant something;
Sunburst something buttocks something balcony;
He frowns at the girl noisily pouring out wine.

245.
In the open-air conclave of scholars he inspects his antique text:
Joy something wine something light something;
Something dancing something eyes something follow;
What is that idiot over there laughing about?

246.
Something something something hands something;
Something perhaps reaches something pineapple;
Better death something love her;
Something something something something giggling.

247.
Something breasts something something bosom;
Something bust something bosom something;
Breast something something caterpillar something;
A look of doubt crosses the old scholar's face.

248.
Death something decrepitude something annihilation;
Something something something rotting putrefaction;
Groans something something shrieks groans;
The old scholar makes a signal to the wine-girl.

249.
Something something something something something;
Something something something smiling something;
Something smiling something something something;
The old scholar finds himself involuntarily smiling.

250.
Despair battle rend heart something;
Grief whatever heaven loss aged;
Thousand miles something tears forgotten;
Smiling to himself, he unrolls a little more of the scroll.

251.
Two stand on a small peninsula, talking of other people's inadequacies;
A small boat has begun to cross the Yellow River tributary;
Halfway across, an alligator attacks it, sinking it;
They fall through the water unworried, knowing this to be impossible.

252.
Three stand on a small peninsula, talking of other people's
  inadequacies;
Horsemen are racing on the other side of the river;
A huge, sinuous hump raises itself above the water;
This worries them more, though they suspect it too is
  impossible.

253.
Pleasure steamers drift down the Chu river,
Past the endless glittering terraces;
The old man looks at them out of the window of the library,
Still pondering the beginning of his autobiography.

254.
The grooms sit back under some trees, relaxing;
High up, on a terraced road, travellers climb and descend;
Even higher, a small wood crowns an impossible pillar of
  mountain;
Even higher up is a rock-face which seems to be falling.

255.
Interesting to compare this picture with its copy beside it;
How a horse rollicking on its back in one
Has become a donkey doing the same in another;
The second groom has a greater expression of surprise.

256.
Through millions of those extremely small irises,
China was perceived, through leaves or falling heights;
Arriving on a branch amid a fluttering of feathers,
Above poets at walls, above masses fleeing in terror.

257.
From behind his tapestried desk the judge frowns
At another miscreant found guilty of incest;
As with severe expression he pronounces sentence,
His daughter is watching him with great interest.

258.
The judge frowns sternly behind his tapestried desk;
Another minor misdemeanour to chastise;
In the waiting-room there has gathered a crowd of millions;
He sighs, remembering when he was still alive.

259.
Having met a sage meditating beneath a tree,
He asked him what was necessary for salvation;
Hearing the exact nature of his reply,
The young man strides resolutely home for an axe.

260.
Welcoming his return, his disciples offer him gifts:
A stone, a toenail, an interestingly warped twig;
His gaze betrays nothing of the turmoil in his heart;
How can he tell them about the woman he met in the town?

261.
Ridge, trees, valley, hills, valley, ridge;
Snow, snow, snow, snow, snow, snow;
Hurrying on to the companionship of the tavern,
He passes between the bodies trapped under the snow.

262.
The four scholars are holding a reunion in a sumptuous garden;
Of the two unfolding the scroll, one looks to the sky;
One leans on a conveniently ledged bend in a tree;
The fourth falls from a branch onto a servant-girl.

263.
The robes of the gathered courtiers point all in the same direction;
A brisk wind blows through the palace pavilions;
After a long absence, the Emperor has returned to them;
Seeing that his sister is still with him, they all relax.

264.
The little girl sits at the table, arranging her hair;
Two older women look towards her inquisitively;
The writing on that assignation was strangely like the
    emperor's;
They recall her mother's disappearance, a year ago.

265.
The game has now reached an exciting stage;
Both of the players are standing on their chairs,
Screaming out insults about each other's mother;
It looks as if a conclusion is within sight.

266.
One of my dreams two nights ago contained a face like that
    Buddhist saint's;
I would so much rather have dreamt about his wife instead;
He was, as far as I recall, involved in painting some sort of
    spacious room;
Now that I look more closely, the resemblance isn't really all
    that striking.

267.
The old monk emerges, smiling, from his meditation;
It was his wish to escape from the snares of the flesh,
And at last the Powers have begun to answer his prayers:
He sees with delight that both his legs have vanished.

268.
He sits in the bed accompanied by four women;
He washes his hands rather abstractedly;
His gaze wanders vaguely to the centre of the room;
The four women try to see what he is looking at.

269.
He sits on the walled bed beside the four noblewomen;
Lying down on his back, he holds up a rare jewel,
Offered to whichever will first sit upon his neck;
The four women watch each other very carefully.

270.
The little servant-girl crossing the floor with a wine-tray
Tries desperately to see who is in the bed in the next room;
By holding her lute delicately upon her shoulder,
A smiling musician effortlessly obstructs her view.

271.
The little servant gyrates lasciviously;
Ignoring her, the monks concentrate on their wine;
Her clapping sister begins to join in the dance;
One of the monks looks up for a moment or two.

272.
The old man is talking to his spiritual adviser;
His spiritual adviser is advising him to leave this house
    immediately;
A little servant-girl passes, carrying a wine-tray;
The religious adviser leaves the house, clutching his face.

273.
She plucks the lute and arches her eyebrows meaningfully;
He cowers away slightly, towards her daughter;
Or perhaps she is his own daughter whom he cowers towards;
At any rate, he cowers slightly towards her.

274.
A cluster of five stand at the back of the room;
One of the three men holds a sturdy stick;
An old man is hiding behind a very large chair;
The woman sitting on the chair smiles nonchalantly.

275.
Glowering out over a room of noise and amusements,
He sits on a large ornate divan, alone;
A woman is standing behind him, looking at him;
She reaches out her hand and then retracts it.

276.
Glowering out over a room full of noise and amusements,
He sits on a large ornate divan, alone;
A woman is standing behind, looking at him;
He broods at the two full tables in front of him.

277.
At the far right of the room, in a recess, a canopied bed;
A single elegant foot is protruding through the curtain;
Nobody in the room pays the slightest attention to it;
After a few seconds, it vanishes again from view.

278.
The young priest has an arm round a small elderly woman;
With the urgency of youth, he plies her with hackneyed
    arguments;
With the wisdom of experience, she gazes fixedly at his throat;
He tightens his grip around her shoulders even more.

279.
The seated man holds her hands, and gazes into her eyes;
She stands in front of him, looking over his head;
The lady leaning on the back of the chair is smiling;
The man standing at the far wall is smiling.

280.
They whisper to each other by a gap in the ornate screen;
He returns to the room to join in a discussion of music;
She returns to her hall to listen to a discussion on Korea;
Quietly she adjusts her slightly disarranged hairstyle.

281.
The Chinese came very close to inventing jazz;
Or, more accurately, to inventing the sort of music
That would sweep through Europe in the 1920s;
But then there were those bad harvests in consecutive years.

282.
A seated woman talks happily to a seated man;
Nearby, a seated woman talks to a seated girl;
A third woman, smiling, strays in from the neighbouring room,
Wondering whereabouts she has left the aphrodisiacs.

283.
Nineteen ladies in all make up the court orchestra;
Assembled together from so many rooms and arguments,
To float harmony across a vast hall towards the Emperor,
Who sits, gripping a forearm, and staring at the third from the
   right at the back.

284.
At first, when the Emperor so avoidably went deaf,
The nineteen ladies of the court orchestra feared they might no longer be required;
But nothing changed, except that now they face away from the Emperor;
He loves the effect of all the backs of those little heads moving in unison.

285.
While the Emperor is listening to his orchestra,
Behind him one of his attendants is talking loudly to a fat woman,
Imagining that the music is drowning out his words;
The expression on the Emperor's face startles some of the musicians.

286.
Seated behind a huge barrel-like hanging drum,
The court lady is cut off from the remainder of the orchestra;
She glances happily out of the window nearby;
At another window a courtier waves a sleeve.

287.
Coming in diffidently to ask a question about the dog,
She sees only her mistress's head lying on the bed;
Languidly its eyes turn to regard her;
She hears a figure running out of the room behind her.

288.
Their fingers tired by hours of delicate embroidery work,
They recline over palace tables in provocative poses;
Some footsteps are heard in the corridor outside;
They look up as the footsteps pass and disappear.

289.
A man is standing among the trees, singing,
And I have to admit I have no idea why he is doing it;
Two women are sleeping together in a nearby inn,
But that is probably a mere coincidence.

290.
The ferryman's boat glides towards the small waiting group;
Quickly they rehearse the main details of their plot;
From the riverside houses such modest groups are seen every
    hour;
Hearing the shouts a little later, they think nothing of them.

291.
I have seen something like this palace in my dreams;
We had left a church near where my secondary school was,
And soon found ourselves among such endless courtyards;
There were such crowds too; but a river, not a lake beyond them.

292.
Finding the funeral monument at the edge of the desert,
He halts reverentially and reads out the inscription;
By the time he reaches the word 'varicose',
He can no longer ignore his giggling servant.

293.
So many birds fly low over the lake;
So many meals still conscious in the sky;
The low sun sparkles in the reeded water;
The occasional arrow wings through the high air.

294.
The mist descends and the valley is obscured;
The mist rises and the village is revealed;
The mist descends and the darkness is revealed;
The mist rises and the valley is obscured.

295.
Fantastical mountains which dwarf the traveller
Are themselves at once dwarfed by the curtain of rock behind;
A single line of water falls thence out of the sky;
Can anywhere on earth be out of sight of this?

296.
Now all the mountain pathways are covered by snow;
They climb sharply through the gully towards the temple;
Halted, shocked, by an approaching thunder,
They watch a tiny snowball trundle past them.

297.
A tributary joins this river at almost every bend;
And in every tributary is a fisherman;
And every fisherman holds a cloth to his face;
And every cloth has been sewn with such great love.

298.
A drumming rain is falling upon the valley;
From his bed the sick man watches the mist rise off the
 temple;
For minute after minute the same rain falls;
For minute after minute after minute.

299.
A curvaceous path at the foot of curvaceous mountains;
It runs straight past a doorway where a man is sitting;
He observes for a moment the passer-by at a run,
But not

300.
He stands stock still in the doorway of a village house;
Seventeen years a soldier in a foreign land,
Yet all in this room is exactly as he remembers it;
Except for the family of Mongolians.

IV

The Moment Passes

301.
Every day the bridge gets a little longer,
And still the people crossing do not notice it;
The old believe it is merely advancing age;
The young believe all sorts of different things.

302.
The little man lying in his well-kept garden
Is not really doing anybody any harm;
His wife sings in the house, and he gives a smile;
He is only imagining doing somebody harm.

303.
Frenziedly he attacks his gasping master,
Chopping off limb after limb with his flashing axe;
The pleasure-steamer drifting past the garden
Goes silent for a while, understandably.

304.
The pavilion commands a superb river panorama,
But he takes advantage of it less and less,
Preferring instead to sit watching the rock-face at its back,
Particularly the area so reminiscent of shoulder-blades.

305.
When the flood screamed down the valley towards the village,
He held up a hand and told it to go away;
It promptly turned aside, coursed over a hill, and disappeared;
That is why that bald, fat man has the wife he has.

306.
After the riotous party, they sail down the lake,
Gathering the debris still floating from the evening before:
A few hats, some torn sheets of paper,
Flowers, a major and a minor poet.

307.
The earthquake shatters the calm of the autumn day;
One moment, lying beneath her, talking quietly,
And the next, falling through the earth unendingly,
While she rises to her knees, and then to her feet.

308.
Since, quite by chance, she discovered that her husband
Was sexually aroused by a small rare orange flower,
She has kept the gardener busy seven days a week.
My God, what a summer this is going to be!

309.
The scholar sits reading in his mountain cottage,
Unaware that, in a town beyond the ridge,
His grandfather has come extremely close to persuading
A woman whom both are fond of to open her gown.

310.
As he strolls in the early morning to investigate a persistent noise,
He discovers his wife kneeling on the grass, devouring his chrysanthemums;
It is at such moments as this that one learns what real love is;
One learns much also about the patterns the dew makes.

311.
Finding the funeral monument at the edge of the desert,
He halts reverentially and reads out the inscription;
Not pausing until he reaches the word 'nucleotide',
When, with a gentle sigh, he rides off into the sand.

312.
The valley is a natural echo chamber;
Although famous far and wide as a recluse,
In fact he lies awake night after night,
Listening to humans whispering to each other.

313.
Carrying tea, the maid hesitates outside the great man's
   pavilion;
She remembers only too clearly what happened the last time
   she went in;
Though hunched over a text, apparently deep in thought,
The great man is already aware of her presence.

314.
The host is weeping; the parting guest is weeping;
The servant is weeping; the boatman is weeping;
Suddenly the guest announces he will stay for a little while
   longer after all;
In the silence, he coughs, and steps into the boat.

315.
Pointing to the ploughmen toiling in the fields,
The nobleman seeks to instill into his son
A reverence for the dignity of manual labour;
Having failed, they go off to view some superb anemones.

316.
It is autumn, and the hermits are migrating;
On the roads leading along the lakes from the mountains
They tramp stolidly, or lie exhausted at the sides,
Easy targets for their natural predators.

317.
The last autumn leaves are descending onto the country road;
Every twenty or thirty minutes, a walking traveller;
Every hour or two, a man on a horse;
Every three centuries or so, a provincial governor.

318.
In their endless halls and echoing corridors,
The Goddesses are re-arranging their gold-based draperies
So that their haunches will be shown to greater advantage;
It seems that a particularly intelligent saint has just died.

319.
The courtyard is full of people who will never die;
None are in any hurry to climb the stairways;
Their every step is as elegant as a dance;
They do not know how much they cannot see.

320.
Towers and pavilions delicately inhabit the sky;
Strange birds descend from the air to rest on them;
They wander among the monks, regarding them curiously;
They shit effortlessly on the prayermats, then fly slowly off.

321.

The little boy eagerly crouches behind the fence,
Watching the three men in the nearby pavilion;
He has never seen people philosophize before;
Somehow he suspects he would rather like it.

322.

The Prince confides his problem to the family doctor;
He listens with sympathy to the description, smiles,
And leaves, on the pretext of finding the perfect cure;
He hurries at breakneck speed to the Princess's quarters.

323.

The Prince confides his problem to the family doctor;
He listens with sympathy to the description, smiles,
And leaves, on the pretext of finding the perfect cure;
A moment later he returns, carrying a hatchet.

324.

Lift up that small flat stone near the mountain-top,
Apply your eye to the aperture disclosed thereby,
And you will see a gorgeously lit palace beneath;
A large guarding bumble bee will then jump on you.

325.

The low shelving rock has some indentations upon it,
Curiously like the impression of a small woman's buttocks,
Which, if they were only properly interpreted,
Would make Geology the most popular subject in the world.

326.
All over the river valley they have met in houses
To discuss the latest reports from the capital:
How can there possibly be a MacPherson Dynasty?
No troubled times could be as troubled as that.

327.
Two monks cross a ravine in the dead of winter,
On their way back to the temple from the village;
No one ever discovered why they disappeared;
Indeed, no one has yet realized that they are missing.

328.
Even half-way up the mountain, there are long valleys,
Which end in instantaneous precipices,
As if the land suddenly remembered its height,
And collapsed in an immediate crisis of confidence.

329.
The woman plods wearily up the mountain path,
Watched by a few bandits behind the trees;
She sighs, and curses under her breath as she walks;
She continues plodding up the mountain path.

330.
The non-existent bird comes timidly out of its nest,
Rather hoping that someone might be passing by underneath;
It is purely the product of the human imagination;
It regards its bleating offspring with equanimity.

331.
A servant-girl is carrying a bowl of flowers,
As she walks along a corridor ahead of a gentleman;
In the evening, a few lights glow in the house,
And the bowl of flowers quivers beside a window.

332.
During his walk, he looks down to his hands,
And discovers there a mysterious, broken-off twig;
Later on in his walk he looks down to his hands,
And discovers there a mysterious, broken-off twig.

333.
Three men are gazing into a curving stream;
Are they, perhaps, looking for the little girl
Who stands behind them, with her hands on her hips?
Or, perhaps, for the woman behind the little girl?

334.
This is the most mysterious of the Palace pools;
The fish are motionless, and the small rocks glide about;
Only the palace children are officially allowed to visit it;
A woman is sometimes there, but no one dares challenge her.

335.
The Emperor is walking along a tunnel
Which links (or so he thinks) his private apartments
With the rooms of a young woman he is rather fond of;
But, unknown to him, he has taken a wrong turning.

336.
The Emperor is walking along a tunnel
Which links (or so he thinks) his private apartments
With the rooms of a young woman he is rather fond of;
His brother is following him at a discreet distance.

337.
There are over a thousand towers in the palace,
And, every morning, another one vanishes;
Tight-lipped officials assemble each day in the Great Hall,
Re-arranging the hierarchy, and swopping rooms.

338.
Ever since the necromancer finally left the district,
Mothers have scrupulously prohibited their daughters
From strolling through the forest where he used to work;
A tree groaning with lust is not a pretty sight.

339.
There is a tense silence in the little garden pavilion;
The monk sits, staring coldly out of the window;
The host, uncertain whether to apologize or not,
Motions his daughter to go back among the plants.

340.
He wakens up with a start, and looks around;
Has he really been sitting like this for the entire night?
Outside, the waterfall still leaps above the temple;
He dares not look round again, in case she has disappeared.

341.
Occasionally, glancing past the head of his talkative host,
To the window of the house visible through the doorway,
He sees a smiling woman's face disappear,
Each time taking slightly longer to disappear.

342.
In the high passes, days drift by without visitors;
Except perhaps for the occasional escaped convict,
Or mystic off in search of further enlightenment,
Or long-lost son, returning with a careful smile.

343.
After uprooting the banana plant, trampling on the chicken,
Decapitating the cock, toppling the statuary
Over onto his host, and demolishing a wall,
He suddenly understands how pointless vengeance is, really.

344.
The crabs emerge quietly from the water,
Cross the beach, dig through a fence, cross a road,
Enter the little pavilion where the scholar sits,
Lift him up, and carry him towards the city.

345.
The old men stand around, aghast and terrified:
The cocks, instead of fighting furiously,
Are entertaining each other with barnyard impersonations;
Doesn't the I Ching say something appalling about this?

346.
With relief, he steps out into the teeming life of the streets;
Never again will he hear that threatening voice;
He stands in the drizzle, watching the hurrying carriages pass;
He can hear the hands moving inside the carriages.

347.
He was expected in the palace half an hour ago,
But still he wanders along a mountain pathway,
Trying to recall the exact expression on her face;
Every so often he breaks off to shout out.

348.
It was the morning when they began their talking,
And now they are still talking, in the evening;
When the sun rises again, they will both be lying
Behind a wall, each with his right arm broken.

349.
In a few seconds, the tea should at last be ready,
A newly invented blend, which, for perfectest flavour,
Ought to be left infusing for seventeen years;
Frequently a widow drinks it by herself in silence.

350.
Seeing the moon, the traveller thinks of home;
Thinks of his young wife lying alone in bed,
Her small hands stroking the place where he should be lying;
He stops his horse, and stares at the full moon.

   351.
In the little pavilion, a woman bends over a table;
A few words are spoken, then a few sighs;
A man lifts his head from a source of fragrance;
Both move slightly, but only very slightly.

352.
Who is the man hiding in the heart of the forest?
And why, whenever a squirrel jumps onto him,
Does he shout out, 'Lun Ai Ngap Ger Tzai Ang Nek'?
Of course, there's an obvious answer, but it's not the right one.

353.
The two brothers sit icily facing each other;
The time for polite civilities is passed;
The old woman gazes wildly from one to the other,
Feeling the grip at each of her wrists tightening.

354.
There are forty-three poets here travelling in a ferry
Designed to carry six passengers safely across the river;
One cannot help wondering whether this administration
Is as sympathetic to literature as it claims to be.

355.
Between the precipitous drop and the sharply sloping forest
Runs a wide snowy track, frequently full of pilgrims,
Moving towards the celebrated tomb at the peak of the ridge;
Millions have come, have admired the tomb, and have gone.

356.
An angry crowd is breaking into a shop,
Infuriated by the standards of contemporary literature;
The owner sits in a locked cupboard at the back,
Hurriedly jotting down a tender memoir of his youth.

357.
At last, after thirty years, he has reached the island,
The little island where his father was born;
He strolls about incognito, asking searching questions,
Unaware of the looks the old women are giving him.

358.
Known throughout the land as the Four Famous Old Men,
The hermits gather together for their weekly meal;
For a long time now there have in fact been five of them;
None of them is quite sure for exactly how long.

359.
The traveller stops to read the placard by the road:
'All pessimists found in this forest will be killed, slowly';
After looking around for a few seconds,
He strides resolutely forward, with a bright smile.

360.
Geese pick a low path along the wooded river,
Sometimes lower than the poets in their pavilions;
The windows are all closed in the river village;
The driving rain hammers against the shutters.

361.
They insist that that island is uninhabited,
But one need only look at it to doubt their veracity;
Not that there are buildings in sight, or smoke, or boats at anchor,
Or wine-shop banners fluttering in the wind.

362.
A smile lights up the exhausted messenger's face;
Beyond a belt of trees he sees the house of the High Command;
All he need do now, to complete his mission successfully,
Is to convince the guard that his horse is in fact a woman.

363.
Beyond the river a volcano is erupting;
He sits on the riverbank, with his back to it,
Placidly admiring the flames reflected in the water;
This man may have taken the delight in nature too far.

364.
Scarcely anyone notices this remote cottage
Pinned tight to the river by hillocks and trees;
There are three murdered bodies lying variously within it,
But even the killer himself no longer returns.

365.
Manfully they fight the river-swell for hours,
Transporting the sick woman towards the city;
The occasional soft moan from beneath a canopy
Terrorizes them more than the clangorous rapids.

366.
Dead leaves befoul the surface of the stagnant pool;
The body of the dead emperor floats beneath them;
The sudden plop of a meteorite disturbs the silence;
Occasionally a stray dog hurries by.

367.
The bird flies slowly back to its remote nest,
Clutching a sheet of paper in its talons,
On which is briefly sketched a superb wide landscape,
Very like the landscape it is flying above.

368.
Half-way up the mountain stands the half-built palace,
Supervised by the half-brother of the Emperor,
Who at present lies half-asleep in his garden,
Head cradled by one of a pair of lovely twins.

369.
A little girl runs screaming out of the house,
Followed, shortly afterwards, by her silent mother,
Followed, shortly afterwards, by her father, talking normally,
Followed, shortly afterwards, by her sister, smiling quietly.

370.
Far below, a fenced road glides silently round the mountain;
For the whole morning he has watched from behind a tree,
Deep into the middle of the afternoon;
Can there really be 48 million people in this country?

371.
In a small cottage past a dilapidated bridge,
Beneath tall sloping trees and unending straight mountains,
Lives one of the two most beautiful women in China;
The second one lives less far away than she used to.

372.
A narrow line of people winds through the burning grass;
A civil war can no longer be avoided;
They carry a few belongings on to other places;
Children in particular, usually still alive.

373.
The hands which planted that flower are no longer here;
They are on the other side of the Yangtse Kiang,
Clasped, white-knuckled, around the handle of a sword;
She reaches out, and draws the flower to her mouth.

374.
A dancing dwarf capers beside the emperor's beloved,
Wondering whether his reputation for insanity
Is well-enough established to let him reach out and touch her;
As a few guards lead him away, he impersonates a tree.

375.
In accordance with a vow he had made long before,
The palace is built on the exact spot where she was standing
When first he caught sight of the woman he knew he loved;
It was just bad luck she happened to be in a cherry-tree.

376.
Every culture possesses some of these smiling old men,
Whom age has filled with a wisdom beyond words;
So much wisdom appears to lie beyond words;
A slight flaw in the cosmic design, don't you think?

377.
Just as the hermit resumes his train of thought,
Another figure comes running through the wood;
Why, after twenty-five years of solitude,
Have three people invaded this forest in the same morning?

378.
An elderly gentleman of distinguished aspect
Is hopping around his garden like a frog;
Some little girls stand up to the waist in the pool;
It takes his mind off the situation in Hong Kong.

379.
From their waists down, they are hidden amid the clouds,
As they walk together across the roof of the mountain;
They cannot see what their feet are moving among;
They are moving among a mountainful of Gods, sleeping.

380.
At his farewell feast, the Ambassador offers a toast,
But carelessly mis-stresses a monosyllable,
Effectively addressing the Emperor as 'Lustbasket',
And undoing the good work of the previous forty-seven years.

381.
The important old lecher smiles towards the harpist;
A second harpist sits motionless by her side,
Wondering why the strings she weakened are not yet broken;
Everyone is smiling, for a different reason.

382.
She slumps on the top of the warming-brazier, lost in thought,
Imagining how she will slump in the bed in the evening;
The servant-girl beside her, even more beautiful,
Looks down at her exquisite hair, and imagines nothing.

383.
They are making more noise than ever they have made before,
As they sit in a clearing in the garden, improvising music;
That bottle of rare old wine has begun to make them deaf;
They break off to drink, laughing louder and louder.

384.
The mynah bird once kept by the great philosopher
And cherished reverentially by his heirs
As unwitting repository for many of his verbal insights
Unaccountably goes missing two days after his death.

385.
The stream staggers over the sandy ground;
The army trudges towards its destination;
A bird feeds its young in the shelter of some grass;
The wind blows a mass of fruit rinds towards the river.

386.
It seems to be less a question of mountains here
Than a giant stone table whose top has been removed;
As he crosses the bridge into the valley,
The back doors of a thousand houses slide open.

387.
This is obviously the perfect spot for a large town;
There is already a superb bridge over the neck of the lake;
A few old men are constructing some smaller shacks;
A sense of expectancy is definitely in the air.

388.
Once more they bid each other a tearful farewell;
Once more they ride around their individual corners
And utterly forget where they are going to;
Tentatively they return and begin to weep.

389.
The fisherboats whip their way through the driving rain;
A man on a mountain path struggles hugely with his umbrella;
A mother shouts at her child to come into the house;
I suspect that very few people have ever understood rain.

390.
With every house he has passed by on this road,
He has heard from inside a cry of 'Don't stop! Don't stop!'
Delivered in tones of obvious ecstasy.
He looks at the sky, suspecting the end of the world.

391.
However desolate the landscape may seem,
It will almost certainly not be utterly deserted;
A distant angler will be there almost hidden by a boulder;
A man will be standing on a bridge, ostentatiously motionless.

392.
The wooden stairway by the waterfall is permanently wet;
On some days, ten people slip on it;
On other days, nobody slips at all;
But always there is water for them to observe.

393.
A steep wall of mountain continues beyond the palace;
An old gnarled tree reaches out over a dizzying drop;
The man in the ox-drawn cart far below is thinking about love;
A few leaves flutter about his head as he drives.

394.
With varying degrees of trepidation,
The three women follow the court official through the palace
    corridors;
Still they do not know which of them has been selected;
A small eager monkey trots along by their sides.

395.
The Emperor is painting the portrait of a little dog;
The little dog gazes querulously to the side,
Then gazes querulously to the other side,
Then gazes querulously straight at the Emperor.

396.
Quite possibly he has foreign blood in him—
The man standing on his head inside the pavilion,
The better to observe the arching waterfall;
It is certainly not the Mandarin way of doing things.

397.
It being a habit he acquired from his father,
To invite his friends to go mountain-climbing with him—
The dearer the friendship, the higher the mountain—
He invites his prospective son-in-law to join him on top of a
    boulder.

398.
A flawless abandoned road snakes its way among the
    mountains,
The legacy of some other forgotten campaign;
Occasionally a panda wanders onto it,
Looks to the left, to the right, and strolls across it.

399.
He opens the door amid the flowering trees,
To investigate the silence in his garden;
His wife has stopped walking, and is looking at the sky;
Smiling, he shuts the door and goes back to work.

400.
China is such a vast country, the little man thinks,
Gazing at the step-by-step diminishing bridge,
Followed by a tiny garden and a little house,
Within which his wife is almost certainly waiting.

V

The Same Laughter, Further Away

401.
He stands stock still in the doorway of his house;
Seventeen years a prisoner in a foreign land,
But only thirty seconds ago his aged father went berserk,
And a fire now blazes in the recognized interior.

402.
Stark bare cedar trees reach arthritically towards the sky;
Pretty inexact, I grant you, but one must make the effort
　　sometimes;
Snow carpets away over the sloping hills;
A young lady is pointing outwards from a nearby wood.

403.
Are those dots people away up on that sheer ravine?
If they are, I suppose they must have some way of getting
　　down;
If they are not people, they may possibly be gravestones;
Which of course is not really a solution to the problem.

404.
The old man gestures; the servant pats the dog;
The donkey ambles; the fishermen dispute;
The volcano explodes; the travellers climb;
The horses graze; the man looks out of the window.

405.
Hurrying over a hill into impenetrable cloud,
Able to see nothing whatever anywhere;
Suddenly, very near, a horse neighing;
The noise of an entire army of peasants marching.

406.
In paradise, a solitary tree grows at the crest of a hill;
Eight or nine old men discuss life in a pavilion;
A little girl stands at the doorway, holding something;
Unlike the others, she seems to be standing on earth.

407.
They pass on the road; the women carried by donkeys,
The men shouldering loads as they move towards a new
    dwelling;
One moves regretfully from a loved house in a village;
The other regretfully moves towards the same village house.

408.
A leaf blows through the empty palace pavilion,
Past the man hiding in a narrow alcove,
On down the corridor, and round the corner,
Past another man hiding in a neighbouring alcove.

409.
A leaf blows through the empty palace pavilion,
Past the man hiding in a narrow alcove,
On down the corridor, and round the corner,
Past a woman hiding in a neighbouring alcove.

410.
By sheer will-power, the monks have induced the twigs to
    burn;
The disbelievers look on, noticeably shaken;
One of them surreptitiously reaches down to his wooden leg;
Finding it warm, he sees the wisdom of conversion.

411.
The bald ascetic grimaces towards the lotus pond;
A podgy servant approaches, carrying refreshments;
Absent-mindedly, the master bites the boy's foot off;
He frowns in vexation as the screams begin to penetrate his dreams.

412.
The sage, with calm, contemplative expression,
Sits back on a high chair which is covered by a cloth;
One finds something of the same style in the occasional nineteenth-century pornographic photograph;
It alleviates the susceptibility to cold leather of the nineteenth-century female backside, I imagine.

413.
The two magpies noisily mock the hare below them,
Secure in what they think is the safety of their tree;
The hare turns his head right round and ponders carefully
Whether or not to pull the string at its feet.

414.
How can so large a river be so high up a mountain?
Can so much rain fall on such a circumscribed area?
I must surely be overlooking something obvious;
From a tiny plateau a huge waterfall descends.

415.
Mist settles deeper and deeper on the small forest;
The leaves continue to flutter to the ground;
Wandering among those childhood trees, looking for his childhood,
He finds instead only a decaying log.

416.
In the first house in the village they are discussing the storm;
In the second house, she lies with her head on the table;
In the third house, they are discussing the storm;
In the fourth house, he sobs passionately to himself.

417.
In the morning after a night of incredible passion,
He walks out towards the peachtree, inhaling deeply;
As he coughs, his right leg falls noisily to the ground;
He hears her calling for him from inside the house.

418.
The emperor is routinely sketching a minuscule bird;
Indifferent to the honour, it dreams of a snail;
The snail is dreaming of an apple-tree;
The apple-tree is dreaming of itself.

419.
Beneath a peachtree, the painter is sketching a sparrow;
The sparrow is dreaming of another bird, now dead;
The other bird dreams of the same peachtree;
The peachtree is dreaming of the painter underneath it.

420.
The emperor lies, dreaming of his daughter;
His daughter kneels, dreaming of a palace guard;
The palace guard stands, dreaming of the tea merchant's wife;
The tea merchant's wife sits, thinking of her husband's bank-
   book.

421.
The emperor lies, dreaming of his palace guard;
The palace guard stands, dreaming of the emperor's daughter;
The emperor's daughter kneels, dreaming of the merchant's wife;
The tea merchant's wife lies, dreaming of the emperor.

422.
The painter sits, drawing a blossoming plumtree;
The blossoming plumtree is dreaming of a denuded orange-tree;
The orange-tree is dreaming of a peculiar apple-tree;
The apple-tree is dreaming of interstellar space.

423.
A dog is pissing against a delicate peony;
The distressed peony is dreaming of a pinetree;
As the dog wanders happily along the forest path,
A pine branch suddenly falls on its head, concussing it.

424.
A dog is pissing against a delicate peony;
The delicate peony is dreaming of an oaktree near it;
The oaktree is dreaming of a coniferous forest;
The forest is dreaming of the rich seams of the earth.

425.
Oh, the emptiness; the challenge of the emptiness;
Inside his drunken head spangles and arrows dance,
As if the edge of the world had fallen away;
No, that is water there; that is water, that is water.

426.
Looking back, they see their path no longer exists;
Is not this how one enters an enchanted world?
The ordinary river eddies at their feet;
As they watch, its surface level gets lower and lower and lower.

427.
Clinging to a servant, he staggers back from the party;
The neighbours, knowing him an austere lawyer,
Are most struck, looking from their various windows,
By the intelligent look on the face of the water buffalo.

428.
As the water buffalo sniffs the grass vivaciously,
The herdboy stares at what he has found by the side of the
    road;
How far could these old arrows travel, he wonders,
Not recognizing the Red Indian markings on its shaft.

429.
A few priests amble across the high stone bridge;
In the distance, at the top of a hill, a pagoda;
They pass an open window, out of which comes laughter;
The screen shuts, and they hear the same laughter, further
    away.

430.
The river cliffs seem to be composed of gigantic slabs;
Surely at any time one of the huge, interlocking components
Might fall back, revealing a glorious world behind it;
The travellers cling fearfully to the side of the boat.

431.
Contentment, as the sage once so wisely observed,
Is to sit by the edge of a mountain lake, gazing down
Through a pass into a mellifluous flowing valley,
While one's beloved is recovering from a fatal illness.

432.
The servant-girl caresses the parakeet;
On the open terraces the lady, smiling, watches her;
Would now be a good moment to tell her the truth about her
    father?
But she hesitates for too long, and the moment passes.

433.
The sweetmeat vendor makes his last sale of the day;
Seventy-three palates gratified by its contents,
He flings the empty tray sullenly into the corner,
Thinking angrily of words spoken by the thirty-first.

434.
The garden terrace is overrun by children;
With what intensity they play their childish games;
One carries another happily upon his back;
The one on his back happily feigns insanity.

435.
Just what exactly are they doing with those insects,
That little boy and girl with their foreheads touching;
If that curiously shaped garden rock were to fall!
How fortunate we are that a picture is only a picture.

436.
The main courtyard of the palace is entirely thronged;
A high balcony within sight of it is almost empty;
No, it is entirely empty, now that a young lady throws herself
    out of it;
No, not entirely empty—there remains a dog barking.

437.
The three scholars glance down as the craft passes;
A small boatman sails serenely by,
Almost hidden behind his cargo of gigantic skulls;
This is the fourth time he has passed this way today.

438.
In a moving display of court ceremonial,
The newly arrived Lithuanian ambassador
Reveals his private parts to the emperor's mother;
Of course, emperors' mothers only pretend to be blind.

439.
A man holding an axe regards two rich passers-by;
One of them appears to be partially covered in snow;
He wonders if they were observing him five minutes ago;
They look at him, wondering much the same thing.

440.
The hermit is in an unusually talkative mood tonight;
At last his chemical experiments have been crowned with
    success;
The neighbouring priest, hearing ever more of the details,
Looks often at the gap in the fence beside the cliff-face.

441.
He reclines on the precipice, looking at the moon;
A straggling pine clings to a perch above him;
One of its cones is falling through the sky;
He hears a meteorite taking off from the moon.

442.
Another of the cones is falling through the sky;
Another of the cones is falling through the sky;
A scholar is silently falling through the sky;
A pinetree is silently falling through the sky.

443.
Half of the huge tree has been snapped off by the wind,
But somehow his light hat has remained in place;
The skiffs batter against their mooring-berths;
Someone else's hat hurtles down the road towards him.

444.
From inside the warm house, they gaze onto the snowy road;
A traveller on a tall horse is passing by;
The recognition is almost immediate:
Only the traveller speaks, softly to the air.

445.
With a burrowing of earth, he emerges from the tunnel;
Early spring; a wet scene; bare willows, distant mountains;
Another of the escapers clambers out to join him;
They shout down to the others not to bother coming out yet.

446.
A moist scene; wet willows; a dank river;
A low damp cottage in a valley of mist;
Even the mountains have another range behind them,
Which is almost certainly only dampness on paper.

447.
He gazes at the moon from the upper pavilion;
She gazes at the moon from the lower pavilion;
A small stairway is all that separates them;
Seeing the moon tremble for a moment, they both gasp.

448.
He gazes at the moon from the upper pavilion;
She gazes at the moon from the lower pavilion;
A small stairway is all that separates them;
A small stairway and a single day.

449.
Ragged, she stands in the snow with naked feet;
It seems as if the otter is not going to return after all;
She should never have given it her jewelry and her shoes;
What is she going to tell her husband when she gets home?

450.
The nobleman on a stag, viewing the lakeside foliage,
Indolent, fanned by an obsequious servant,
Expires, the cruel victim of mistaken identity,
When a woman appears from the water and fires and arrow at him.

451.
Four swallows float beneath a brief band of landscape,
And ten Chinese characters float in the sky above it,
Seeming even more birdlike than the swallows,
Or an urgent message from the God of the Sky.

452.
Snoozing happily in a drifting bark,
He sees mist rise and fall from the mountains opposite,
In the exact profile of his late wife's face when passionate;
But surely she fell to her death from quite another place?

453.
All the valley trees seem angled and tortuous,
But a straight tree stands at the sharp coned peak of a
    vertiginous mountain;
Somebody has broken the little fence by the riverside;
Doubtless by falling through it, obsessed by the high straight
    tree.

454.
Returning from a soothing walk in the hills,
He discovers that his house has been stolen during his absence;
A few lost planks lie scattered in the cabbage patch;
His wife stands by the river, smiling nervously.

455.
Sailing quietly round the back of the little island,
He finds his path thwarted by an undeniable neck of land;
At home, all his brothers tell of the same thing happening;
Their father nods sagely and expounds to them the remedy
    for this.

456.
A small stream trickles through a peripheral valley,
Watched by a man leaning against a tree;
At a certain point he walks away from the tree;
The stream continues to trickle through the small valley.

457.
All day, they drag the misty river, searching for her corpse,
Round corner after corner of its reedy shallows,
Discovering only twenty or so different men,
Each with a roughly similar smile on his face.

458.
Surely this looping stream was straighter yesterday?
He looks down to the little trap of rocks below him;
The bottles which he emptied yesterday are still caught there,
    and float;
Or was he facing the other way yesterday?

459.
Surely this looping stream was straighter yesterday?
He looks down to the little trap of rocks below him;
The bottles which he emptied yesterday are still caught there, and float;
Or was I facing the other way yesterday?

460.
And yet, the Chinese never invented skis, or did they?
Otherwise, surely, those two, laboriously carrying loads along that pathway,
Underneath such sheerly invitational slopes,
Would have been assailed by the merry warnings of skiing noblemen.

461.
Only after seventeen years did the mist totally lift
From that dainty inlet with its house and clumps of trees;
And he found himself gazing from his paralysed window
At another dainty inlet with a house and clumps of trees.

462.
There seems no reason why mountains such shape should stop;
Their summits seem unnecessary concessions;
Yet, just when the sky is about to surrender to them,
They abolish themselves in a field of ordinary trees.

463.
That morning, the tree finally lost its patience;
Branches closed firmly round the wine-arbour and threw it into the distance;
No more would it vibrate to maudlin songs about their homelands;
As a precipice flies by them, the carousers pause in their singing.

464.
Three of the scholars sit, examining documents,
While a fourth stands, with his lips around a young girl's nose;
He claims it is an infallible aid to memory;
After an hour, they lightly jog his shoulder.

465.
The last commentary has been completed
On the sexual autobiography of a long dead civil servant;
One of the scholars sombrely dances on the table,
But the rest sit staring vacantly into space.

466.
After such a journey, after so many great cities,
To have crossed great river after great river,
And now, on a rickety bridge, among snow and small hills,
To be approaching a single house ever more slowly.

467.
The wild river a mass of chaotic currents,
With calmness they negotiate the fatal rocks;
As they pass one on which a young girl sits,
They remember the pilot's warning, and burst into song.

468.
With ritual pomp they prepare to return to China;
They drain their glasses as a keen wind hurries the trees;
To symbolize their faith, they bite off a sparrow's head;
As the freed rabbit runs past, each tries to kick it.

469.
With ritual pomp they prepare to depart from China;
Blindfold, the guides crawl backwards between great fires;
The hypnotized camel topples onto its side;
Slowly each head immerses in a bucket of water.

470.
She has come back, at last she has come back!
On the main street, a crowd coagulates to greet her;
From a high window, a watching lady scowls;
Outside, two former friends ignore each other.

471.
She rides with stately ease, holding one of her children;
The Governor has kindly provided her with a soldier for escort;
He rides alongside her, holding her other child;
For mile after mile she seeks to avoid his gaze.

472.
She rides with stately ease, holding one of her children;
The Governor has kindly provided her with a soldier for escort;
He rides alongside her, holding her other child;
For mile after mile, he seeks to engage her eyes.

473.
From where he looks, trees cut the road into sections;
In one of these strips, two men gesticulate wildly;
Three other ribbons are mere slices of nothingness;
In another space he watches a woman dancing.

474.
This mountain seems to widen towards its top,
And gorgeous temples occupy its wide plateau;
He is obviously a demented anti-clerical
Who hacks with a hatchet at the thin mountain base.

475.
He edges nearer to the escaped horse,
Holding out a tempting sample of succulent hay;
Though the horse leans back, it stretches its nose forward;
In its hoof it holds out tempting pictures of women.

476.
Looking apprehensive at the centre of the procession,
She is brought to be married to the stupidest emperor in all
    Chinese history;
Yet already that evening, from the way he falls out of the
    bed,
She foresees that their life together will be perfectly tolerable.

477.
For forty-seven years he has disdained the company of men;
He walks to the entrance of his cave and looks down to the
    village;
No, no, they would only look at his ears and laugh;
Slowly he walks back into the depths of his cave.

478.
In a rage he tears up the holy manuscript,
Which sought to prove, at great length, that everything is
    illusion;
Scraps of precious wisdom flutter down the mountainside,
Creating the illusion of a flight of snowy egrets.

479.
I remember I once cut this image out of a French magazine,
Li Po, once enclosed in the dream of a great poet,
Which now I suddenly re-encounter among unseen landscapes;
Or rather, this imagined portrait of what he looked like.

480.
Calmly approaching the mountain pass in deep snow,
His gaze settles on a solitary clump of trees;
Surely he dreamt once of being hanged from such a cluster?
He smiles towards the companion riding beside him.

481.
In every cave, it seems, someone is meditating;
I mean, what good is it doing anyone else?
In a flash, the mountain disintegrates to nothingness;
Travel to the coast suddenly becomes much easier.

482.
She emerges sadly from her meditation,
Disappointed by its failure to achieve anything;
She turns to ask the servant beside her to fetch some water,
Puzzled at first to find in her place a flower in a vase.

483.
The trees are broken, and the bridge has rusted,
And all the laughter is in previous dynasties;
Each night the rivers grow a little narrower,
And every morning they grow a little wider.

484.
After he has finished painting the monkey,
She ambles towards him with her hand outstretched;
Taking the brush from him, with a few swift movements,
She sketches in the background a wheel rolling up a hill.

485.
He lies awake, listening to the night rain;
How it calms his heart, with its quiet, impersonal music;
In fact, a man-eating tiger is also out there, pissing sporadically;
He caresses his wife's profile, sleepless but happy.

486.
The bird stands on a convenient ridge in the pine-trunk;
Absolutely none of the others has turned up;
He mutters to himself, feeling pretty basely betrayed;
The next time, things will certainly be arranged differently.

487.
Their swords clash by the cottage beside the lake;
Hearing the sound, the peasants run swiftly towards it;
They arrive to find not the least sign of a struggle;
The severed head smiles underneath the water.

488.
Seeing the reflection of the moon shimmering in the lake,
He looks far up, his arms round his beloved;
Nowhere in the sky can he see the moon itself;
He feels inside her mouth for it, also unsuccessfully.

489.
What depths the wild geese suddenly give the skies;
With what precision they marshal in immensities;
Neater perhaps than your thoughts, but no nearer;
Deep in the sky, no deeper than your eyes.

490.
With increasing bonhomie as the afternoon progresses,
They slump beneath the willow, exchanging sexual exploits;
The smaller man describes a strange example of pubic hair
   which he once saw;
The older man lurches unsteadily to his feet, shouting.

491.
Totally drunk, they emit the same giggle;
Pointing, one describes delightedly the parts of the other's
   wife;
Delightedly, the other does the same for his companion;
On the following morning, both lie awake, thinking.

492.
The meditative monk inhales the weed reflectively;
In his mind's eye, he sees a quiet street in a town,
Where he would like to settle in his declining years;
On the walls there would be pictures of water buffaloes.

493.
He gazes out of the window on a quiet afternoon;
Five dragons in the sky are tearing each other to pieces;
He asks his wife to come over and look at them;
Still spinning in circles, she complies with his request.

494.
The climbing vine that grows against his wall
Imitates exactly the branching of his veins;
Absent-mindedly tearing at a stalk one morning,
He remembers a cruel phrase he once used to his mother.

495.
The climbing vine that grows against his wall
Imitates exactly the branching of her veins;
Absent-mindedly tearing at a stalk one morning,
He hears a shriek from the bed he has just left.

496.
They had cause to thank the inquisitiveness of fish,
Though the marks they made changed less slowly than their
 own skin;
Their happiness once grew out of the ground,
And for a while they could watch their women's mouths
 opening.

497.
I have no more to say about dancing-girls;
I have no more to say about archways and emperors,
And the same divinities repeated a thousand times;
What an enchanting face that woman has.

498.
Eight old men walk solemnly along the riverbank;
Behind them a sad woman carries a folded chart;
On closer inspection, I can see that some of the eight are
 women too;
Will there be anything more interesting over the page?

499.
Eight old men walk solemnly along the riverbank;
Behind them a sad woman carries a folded chart;
On closer inspection, I can see that four of the eight are
 women too;
I close the last book, and open and close my eyes twice.

500.
A day or two later, in the library again,
The place full of students studying Van Gogh and such,
I notice the seven big red volumes standing untouched upon their shelf,
As they did for so long before, curious, I looked into them.

501.
The ancient pagoda has finally been deserted;
All the young have drifted away from the small island,
Leaving it only with its euphonious name;
I wish I could remember what its name was.